NORMAN BRIDWELL
Clifford's
ABC

scarecrow

elephant

dog

elf

ISBN 0-590-40453-9

Copyright © 1983 by Norman Bridwell.
All rights reserved. Published by Scholastic Inc.
CLIFFORD and CLIFFORD THE BIG RED DOG
are registered trademarks of Scholastic Inc.

16 15 14 13 12 11   9/8 0 1 2 3 4/9

Printed in the U.S.A.

NORMAN BRIDWELL

Clifford's
ABC

alligator

beaver

cow

SCHOLASTIC INC.

New York Toronto London Auckland Sydney

Aa

accordian

axe

armadillo

anvil

acorns

ant

anchor

alligator

Bb

bird

ball

bat

boots

basket

balloon

boy

boat

butterfly

beaver

bottle

baby

Cc

Cc
cactus
cake
candle
cape
cat
checks
clown
collar
cook
cow

collar

cow

cat

cook

candle

cake

cactus

clown

checks

cape

Dd

dragon

dolphin

dog

dummy

derby

drum

dandelion

eagle

egg

Ee

earring

elephant

elf

Eskimo

eel

Ee
eagle
earring
eel
egg
elephant
elf
Eskimo

Ff

frog

fly

flag

fish

fire

fairy

flea

funnel

flower

fox

ghost

giraffe

gorilla

garden

goat

Gg
garbage can
garden
ghost
giraffe
glove
goat
gorilla

glove

garbage can

Hh

helicopter

harp

house

horse

hollyhock

hummingbird

hat

horn

ystack

hippopotamus

Ii

Ii
ice cream cone
igloo
iguana
ink
iris
iron

iguana

igloo

iris

ink

ice cream cone

iron

Jj

jet

juggler

jogger

jack-o'-lantern

jester

jacks

Kk

kangaroo
karate
kayak
kitten
knight
knitting
koala

Ll

lamb
lasso
leopard
lily
lion
lobster
log
lumberjack

Kk

Ll

koala

knight

lobster

lily

lasso

karate

lumberjack

knitting

kitten

log

kangaroo

kayak

leopard

lamb

lion

Mm

moon

mop

map

monkey

mask

mittens

mouse

magician

marionette

magnet

Nn

note

nest

net

nun

nutcracker

nut

nurse

noodles

Oo

owl

orchid

ostrich

octopus

orange

overalls

oar

parachute

pineapple

palm

picture

panda

pirate

paintbru[sh]

pear

palett[e]

pony

pig

porcupine

P

Pp
paintbrush
palette
palm
panda
parachute
pear
picture
pig
pineapple
pirate
pony
porcupine

Pp

Qq

quail

artet

quartet

question

queen

quilt

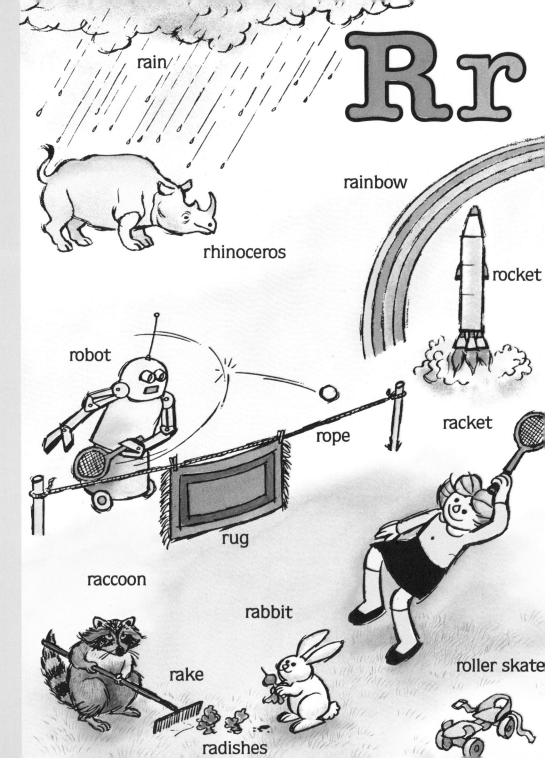

Rr

Rr
rabbit
raccoon
racket
radishes
rain
rainbow
rake
rhinoceros
robot
rocket
roller skate
rope
rug

rain

rainbow

rhinoceros

rocket

robot

rope

racket

rug

raccoon

rabbit

rake

roller skate

radishes

Ss

Saturn

star

scarecrow

sleep

soccer ball

saxophone

sausage

seesaw

sandwich

squirrel

snail

seal

stool

Tt
table
teapot
teddy bear
telescope
television
tent
tepee
tiger
tractor
train
turtle

Tt

tent

tepee

tractor

tiger

telescope

televisi

teapot

train

teddy bear

turtle

table

Uu

umbrella

UFO

unicorn

umpire

urn

ukulele

unicycle

Vv

volcano

vampire

valentine

viole

vise

violin

vacuum cleaner

vase

Ww

whale

waves

walrus

wrenches

wheelbarrow

witch

wolf

worm

waffles

wagon

W

Xx

Yy

xylophone

yacht

yak

x-ray

yawn

yarn

yo-yo

Xx
x-ray
xylophone

Yy
yacht
yak
yarn
yawn
yo-yo

zeppelin

Zz

zebra

zipper

zither